The Tiniest Acorn

A Story To Grow By

Marsha T. Danzig

Frederick Fell Publishers, Inc.

For information, please write: Frederick Fell Publishers, Inc.
2131 Hollywood Blvd., Hollywood, FL 33020

First edition published 1999
1 3 5 7 9 10 8 6 4 2

Library of Congress Cataloging-in-Publication Data
Danzig, Marsha, 1962 -
     The tiniest acorn : a story to grow by / Marsha Danzig.
     p. cm.
     ISBN 0-88391-001-2
     1. Acorns - Fiction. 2. Oak - Fiction.
     3. Growth - Fiction. 4. Self-confidence - Fiction. I. Title
     P27.D2393 Ti 1999
     E - dc21   98-37760
                                       CIP
                                       AC

BOOK DESIGN BY
Don Morris Design

ILLUSTRATIONS BY
Matthew B. Danzig

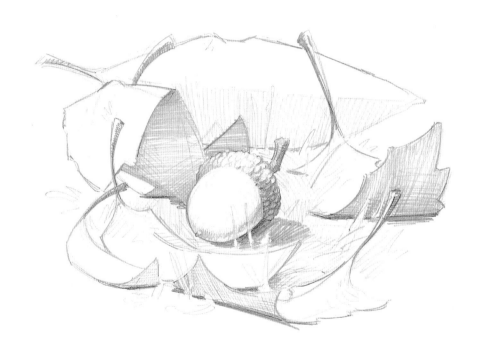

Once upon a time there
was a tiny acorn named Lulu.

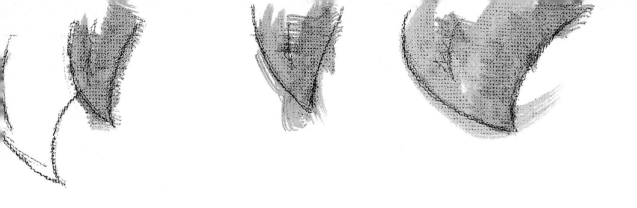

She was so small that hardly
anyone noticed her as the wind
blew her from place to place.

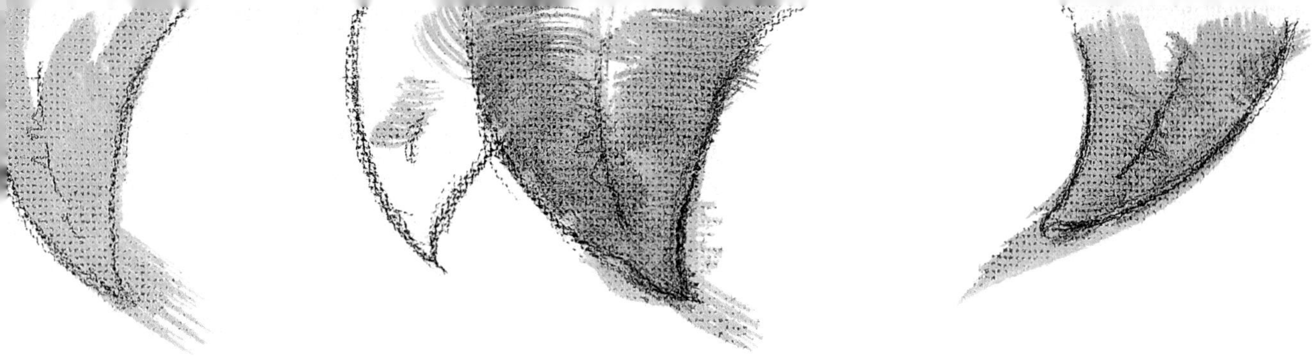

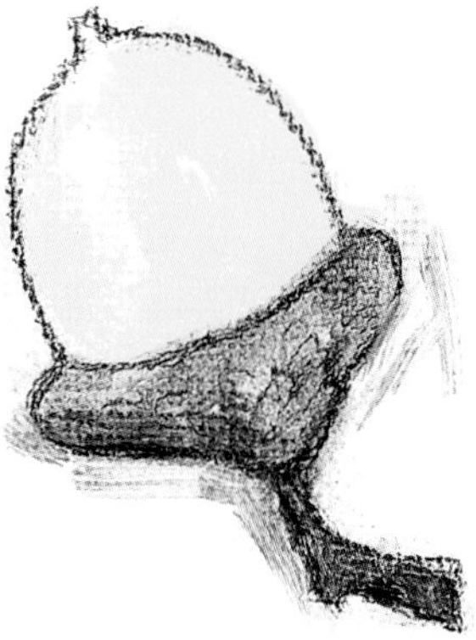

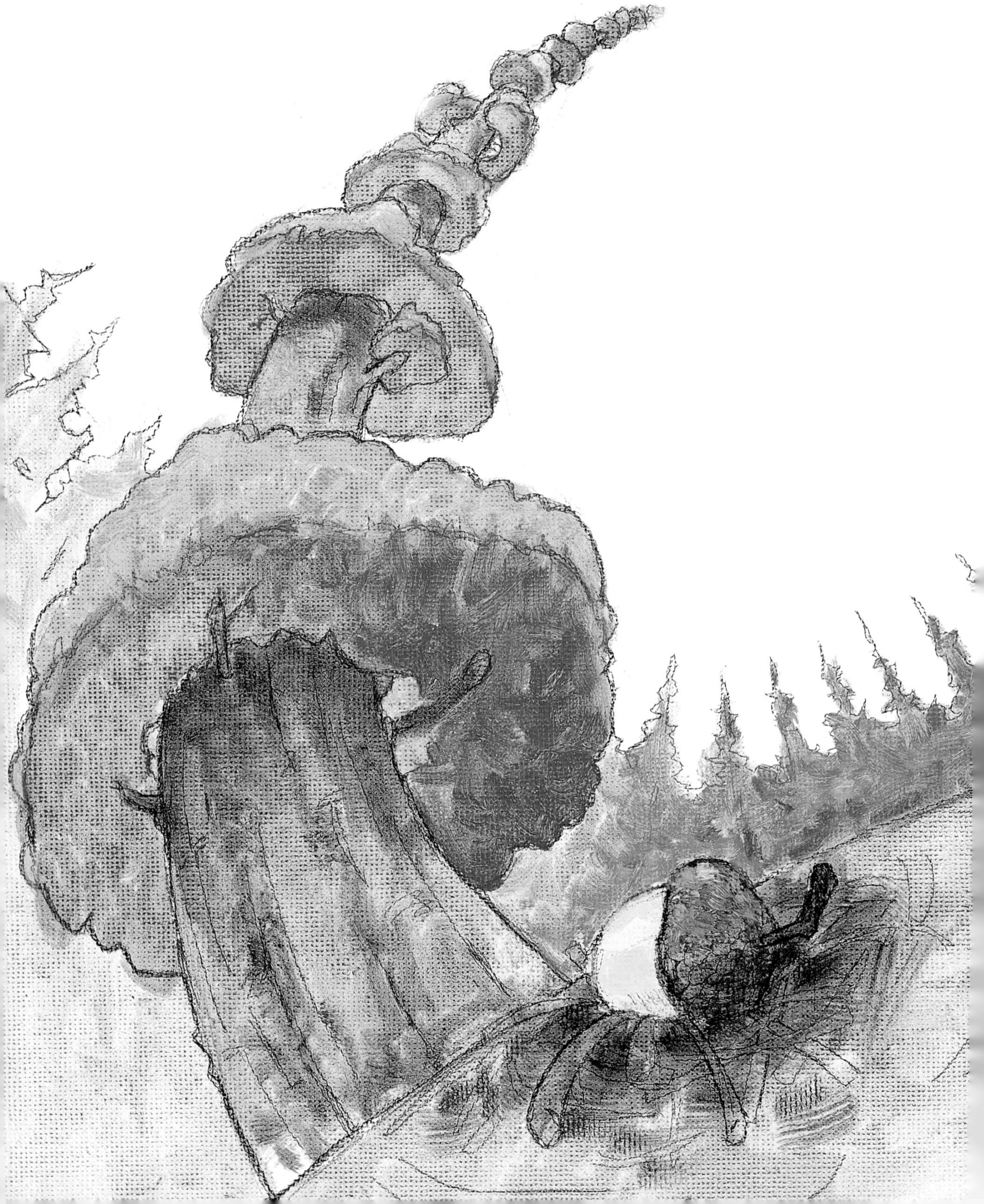

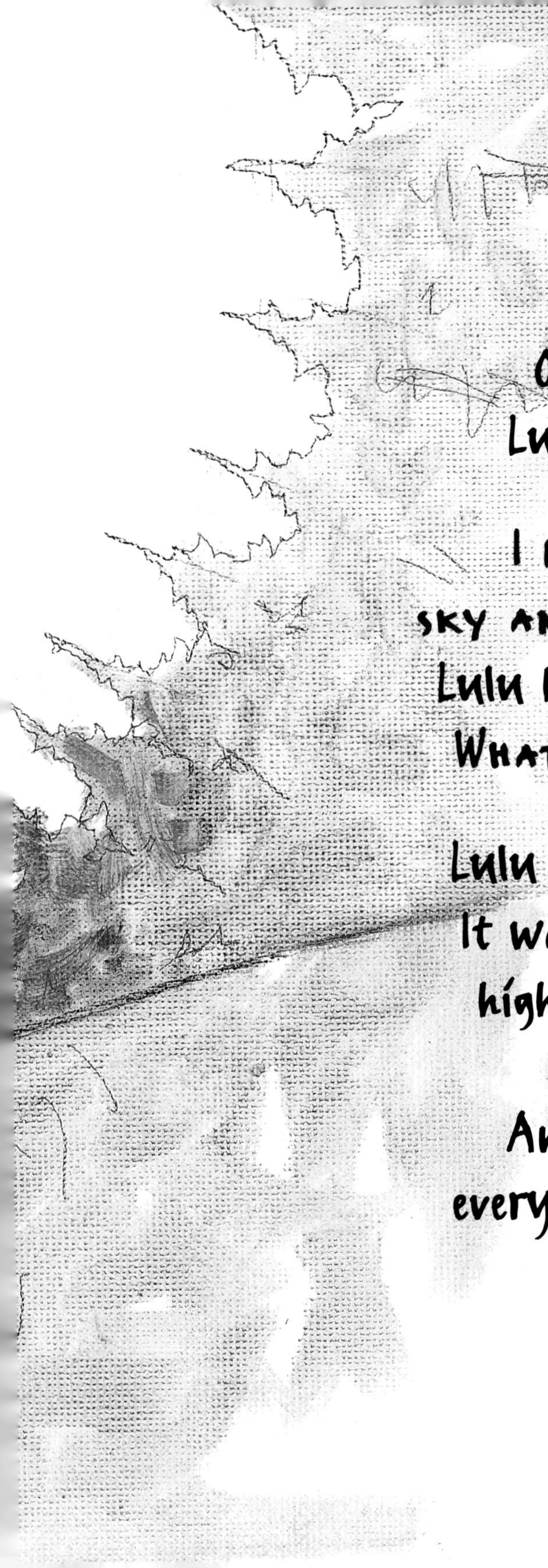

One day the wind blew
Lulu into a tall pine tree.

I REACH HIGH UP INTO THE
SKY AND SHADE EVERYTHING BELOW,
Lulu heard the tree proudly say.
WHAT CAN YOU DO TINY ACORN?

Lulu looked up at the pine tree.
It was true. The tree did reach
high into the sky—it almost
touched the clouds.
And, its shade did protect
everything below from the sun.

Before Lulu had time to
think what she could do,
a strong wind came and
swept her into a field of daisies.

WHAT CAN YOU DO?
the daisies asked as they
swayed in the wind and
brightened the field.

Lulu thought and thought.
She did not know what
she could do. But, just
before she was
about to give up,
the wind stirred again.

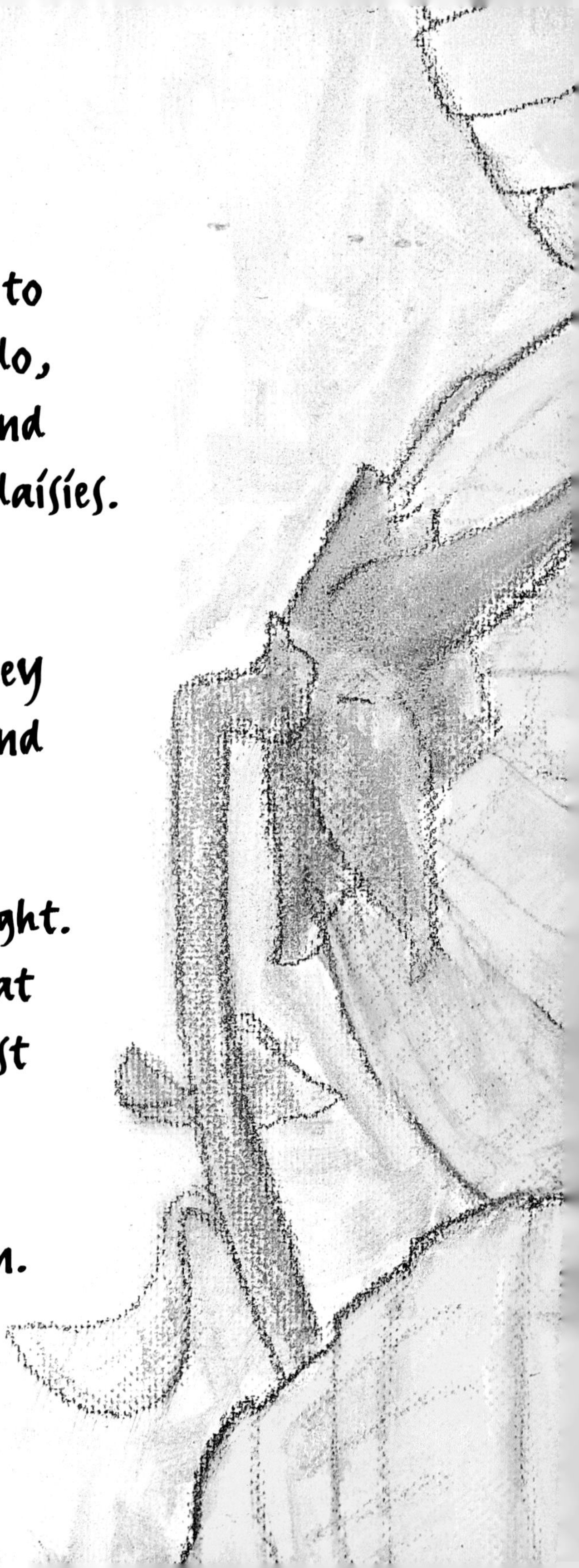

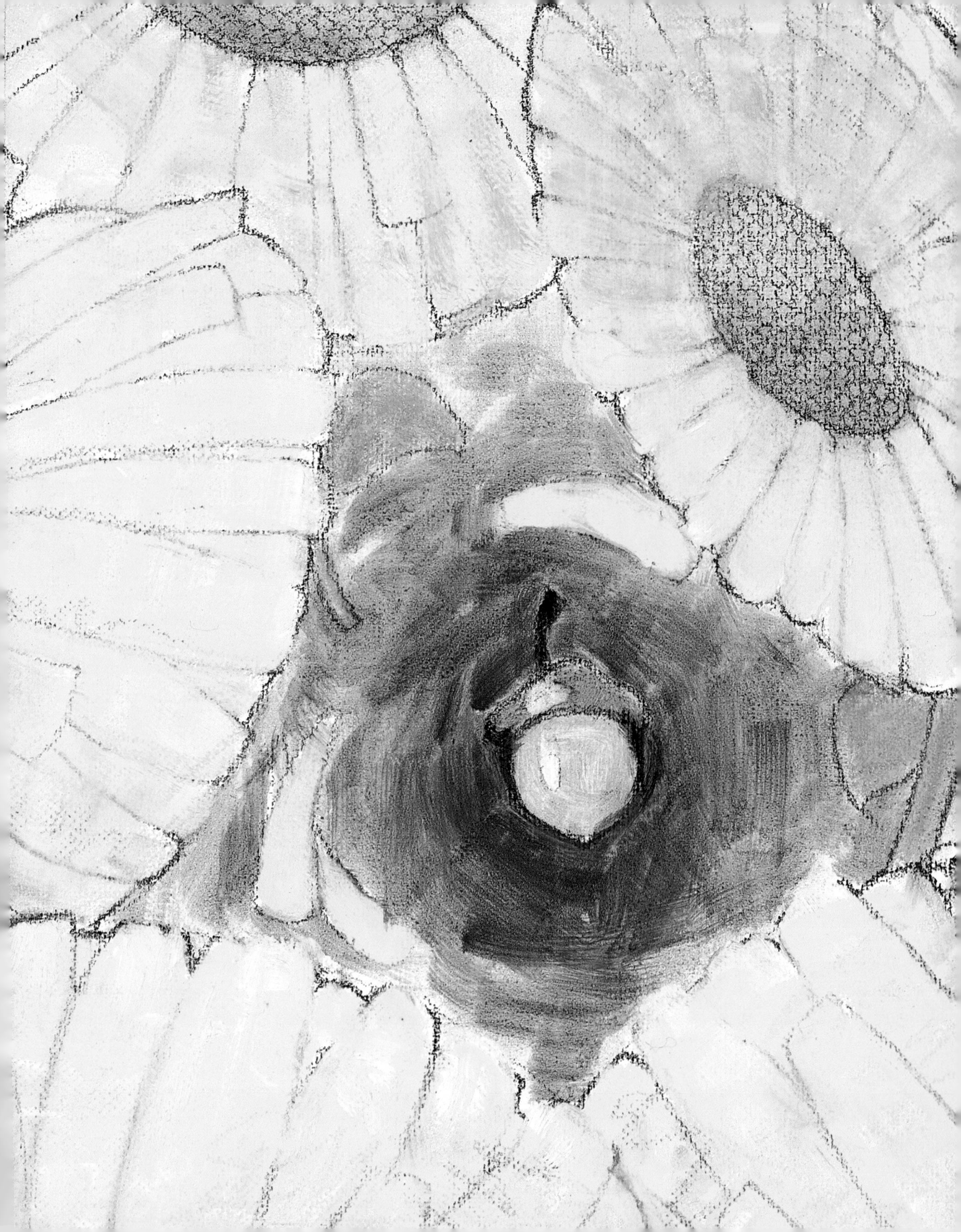

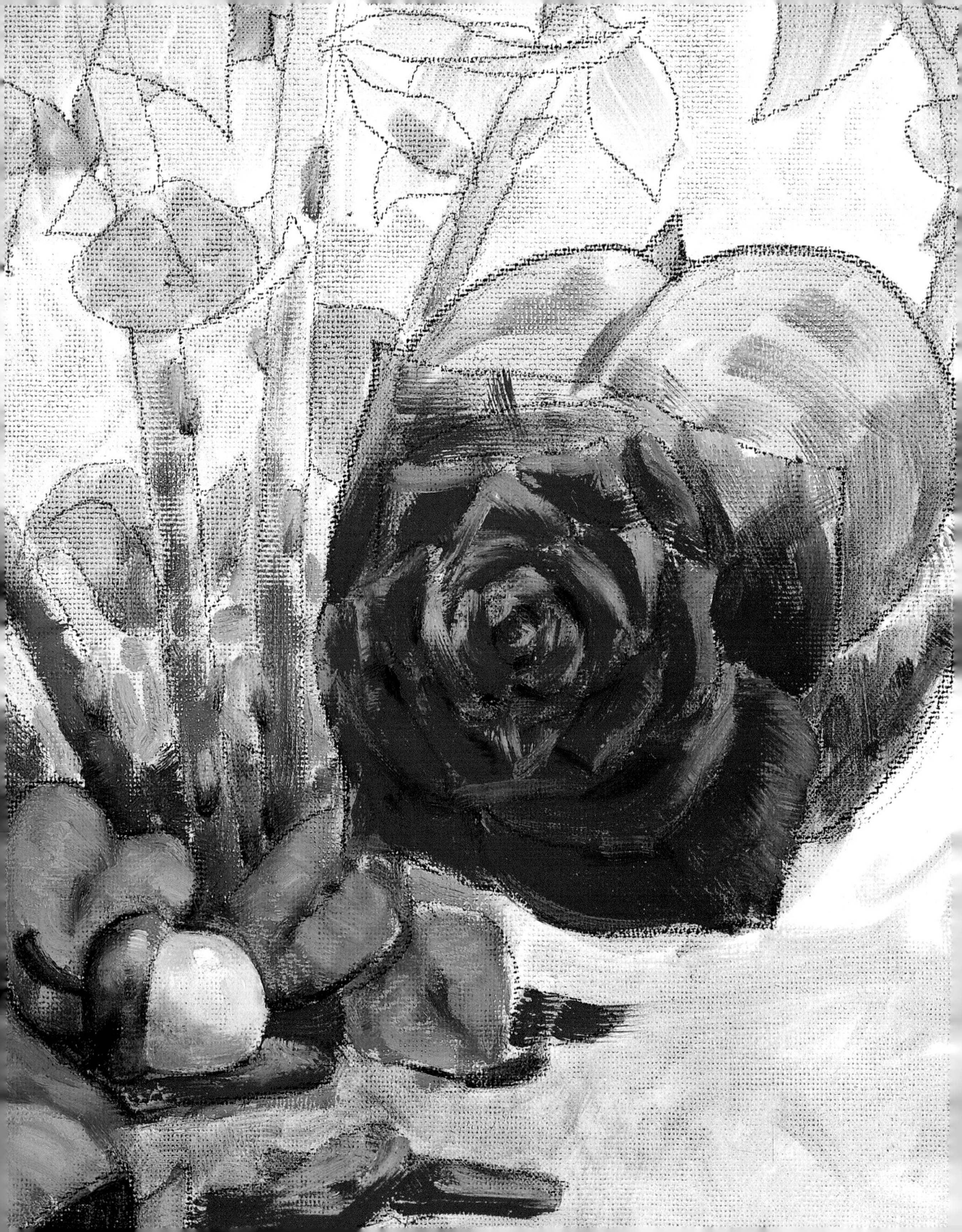

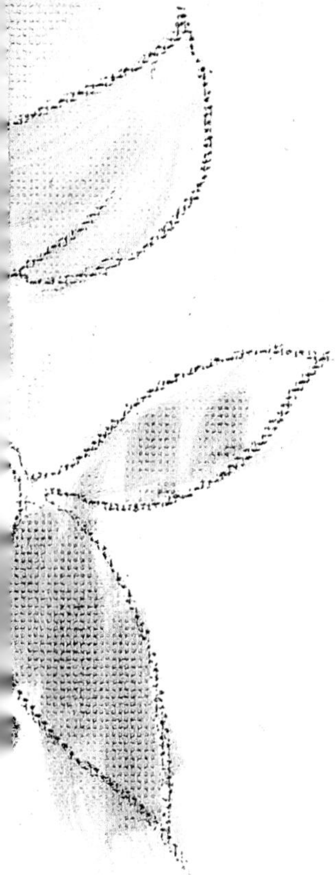
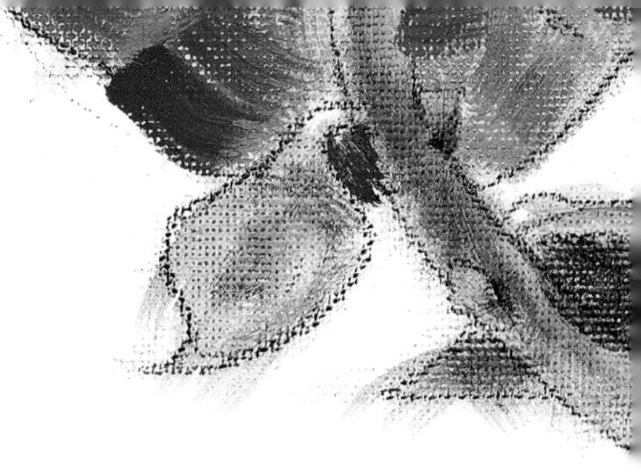

This time a single rose
saw Lulu blow in.

I AM THE MOST BEAUTIFUL
FLOWER IN THE WHOLE WORLD,
AND I SMELL SO SWEET
I PERFUME EVERYTHING AROUND ME.
WHAT CAN YOU DO TINY ACORN?

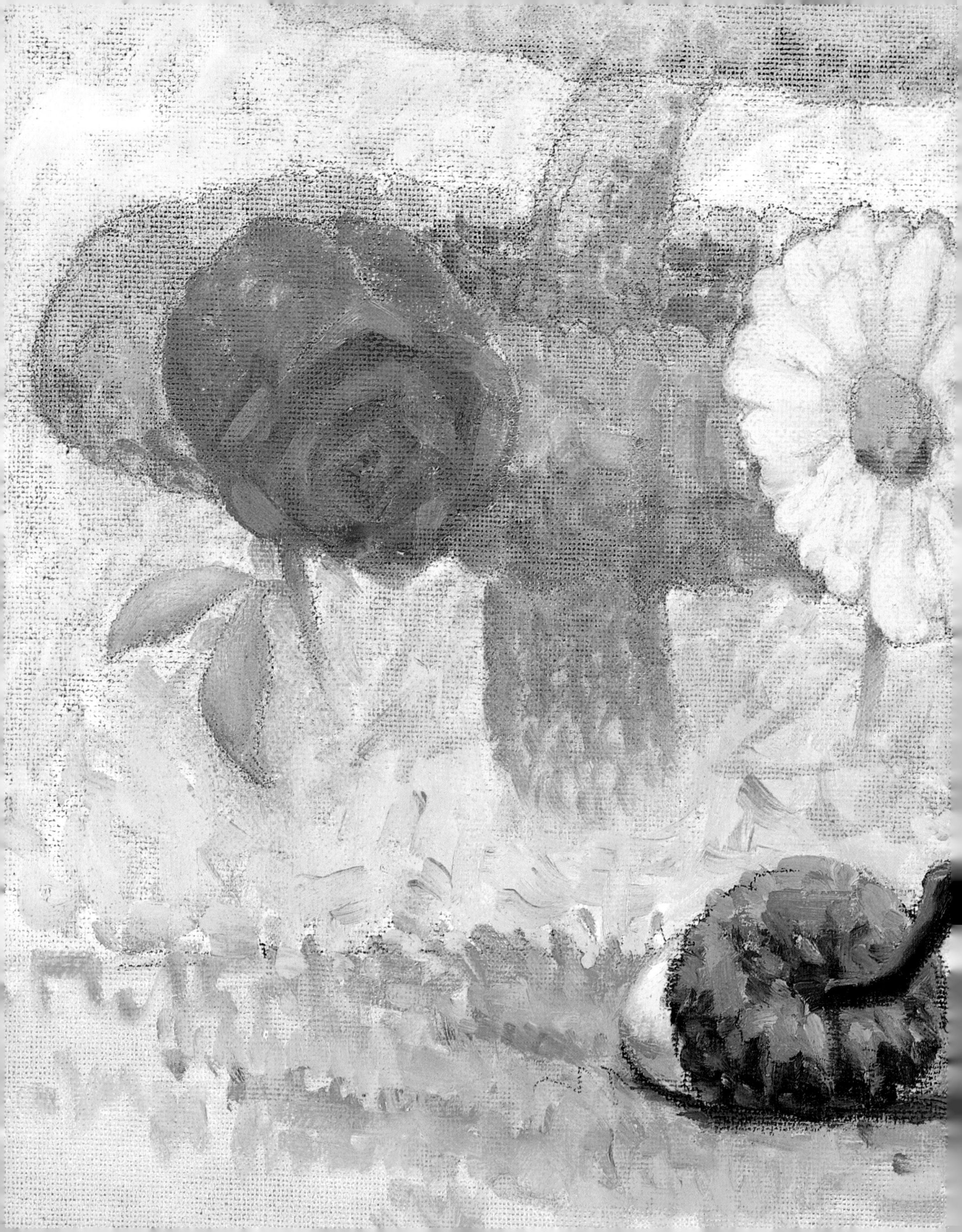

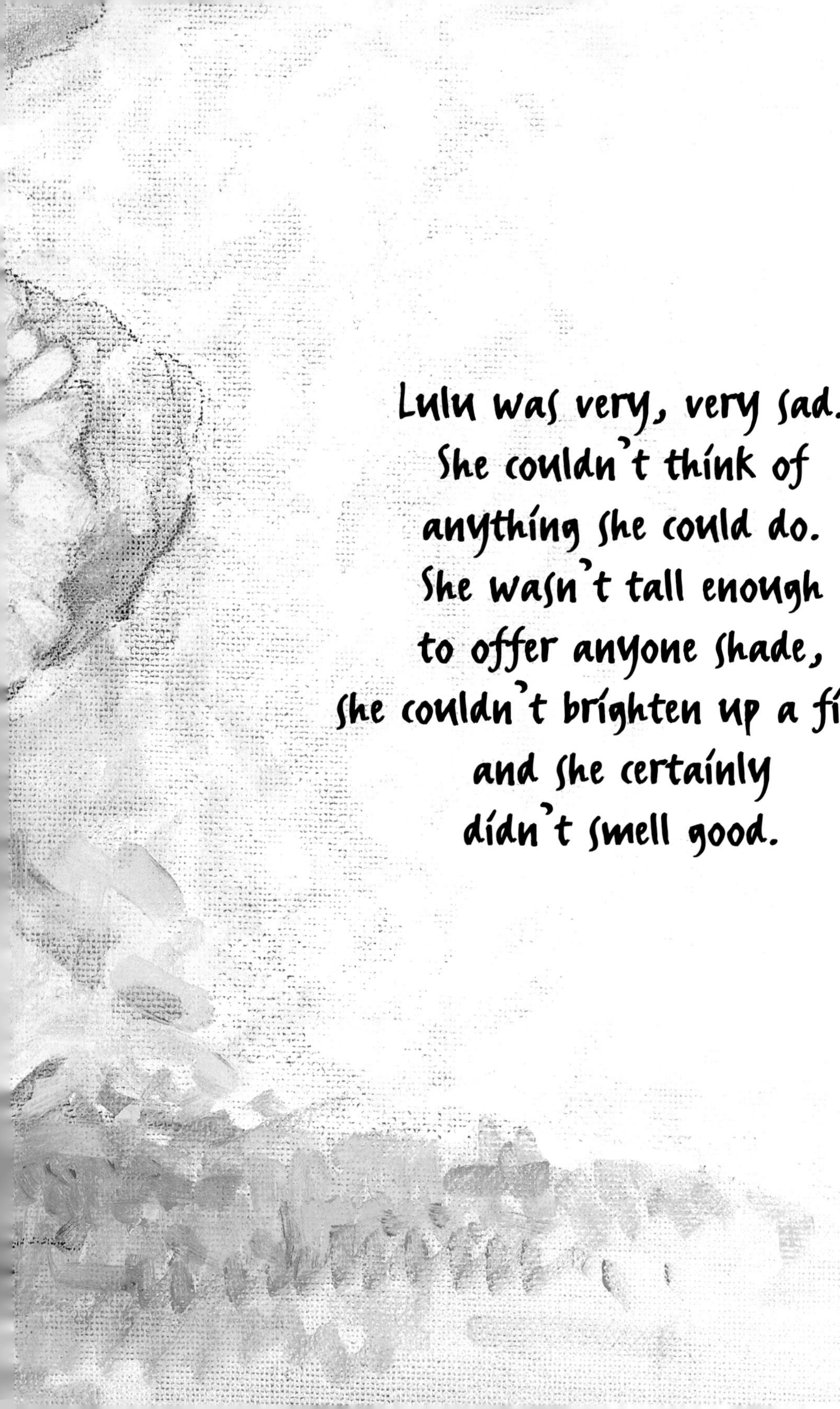

Lulu was very, very sad.
She couldn't think of
anything she could do.
She wasn't tall enough
to offer anyone shade,
she couldn't brighten up a field,
and she certainly
didn't smell good.

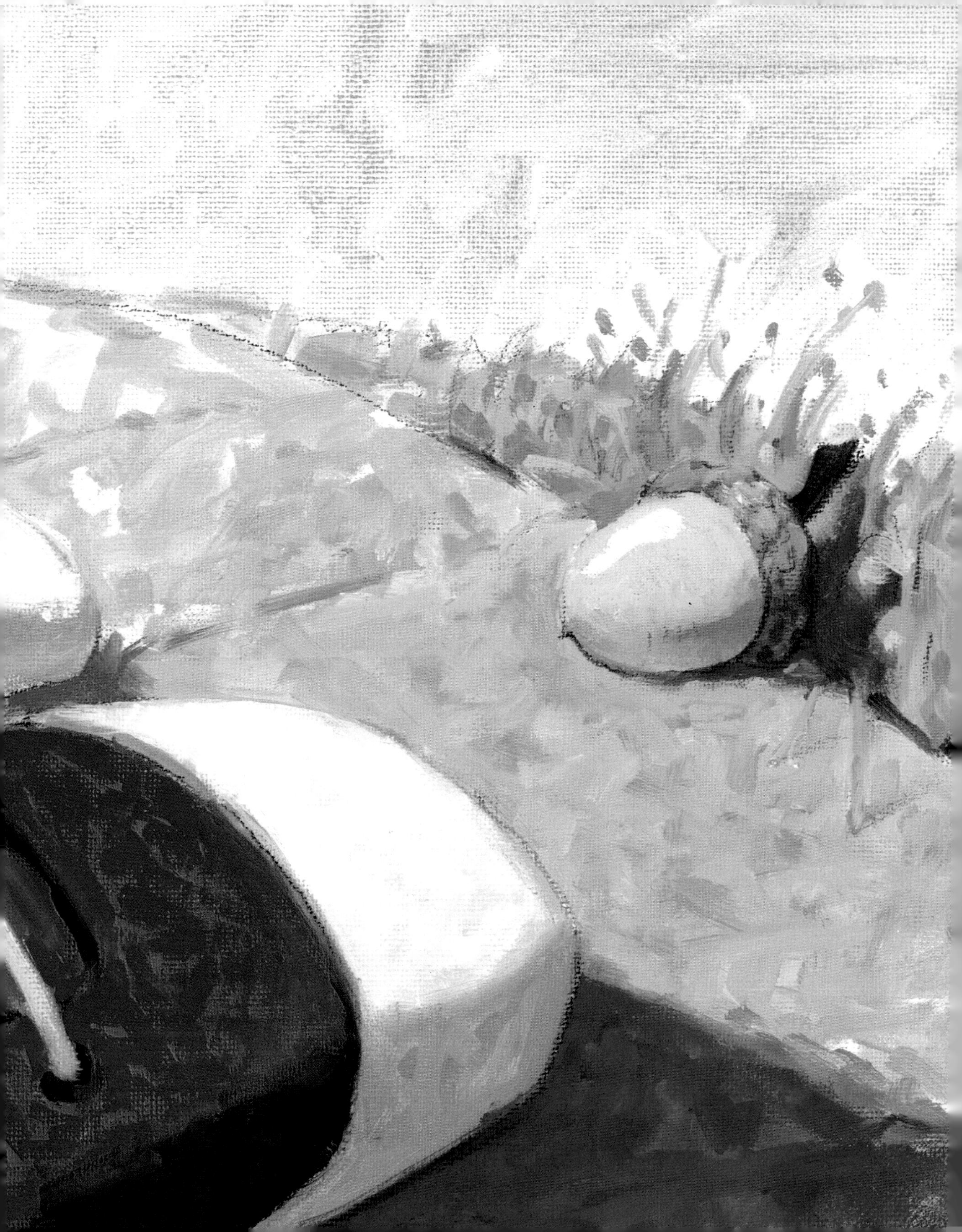

Soon the wind came
along again, this time
in a strong burst that
sent Lulu spinning through
the air. Lulu finally
came to rest on a hard
sidewalk. After a few
minutes, a young boy
came walking by.

When the boy picked
Lulu up and said,
WHAT A PRETTY ACORN,
Lulu was surprised!
HE MUST HAVE MADE A MISTAKE,
she thought. HE COULDN'T
POSSIBLY BE talking ABOUT ME.

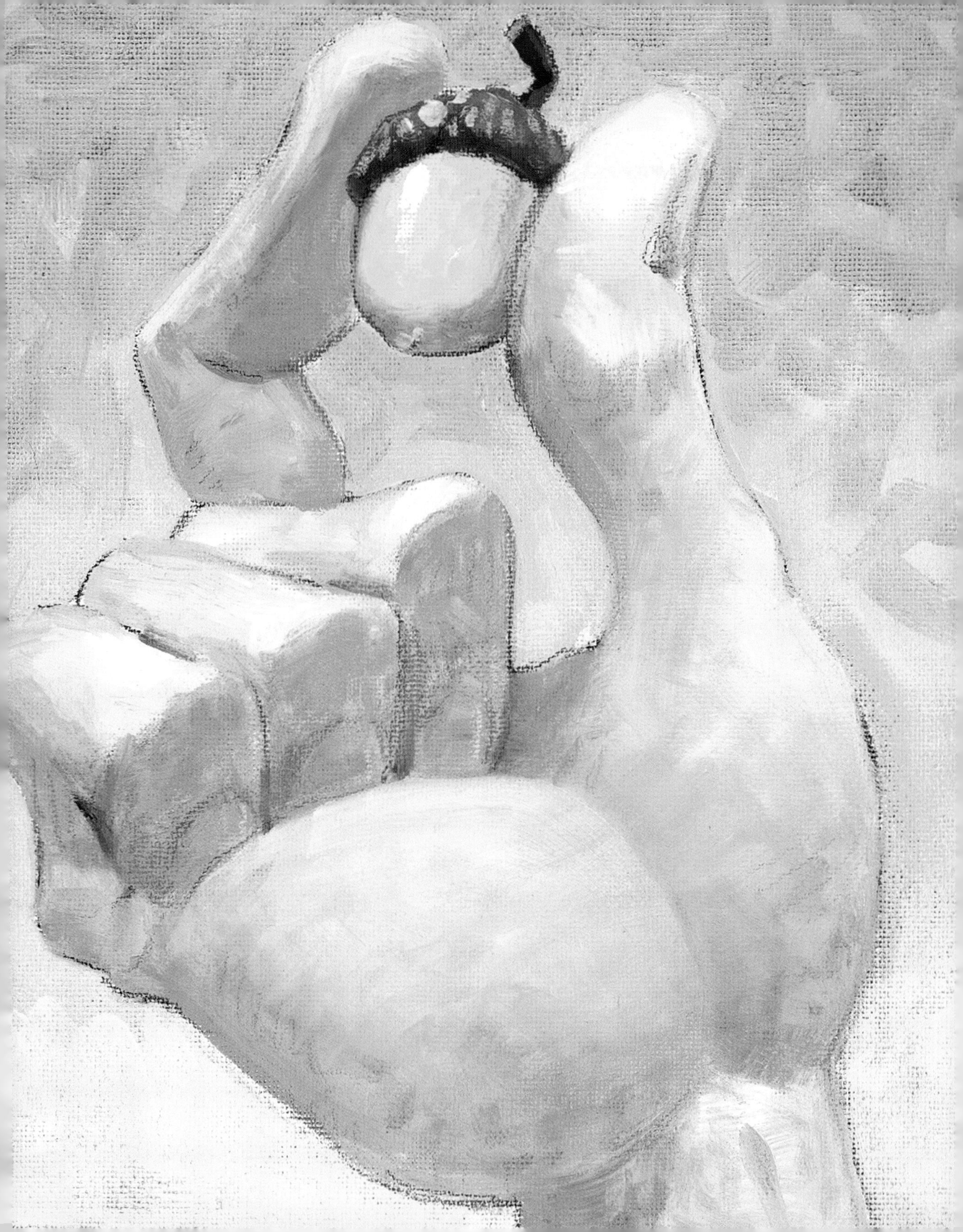

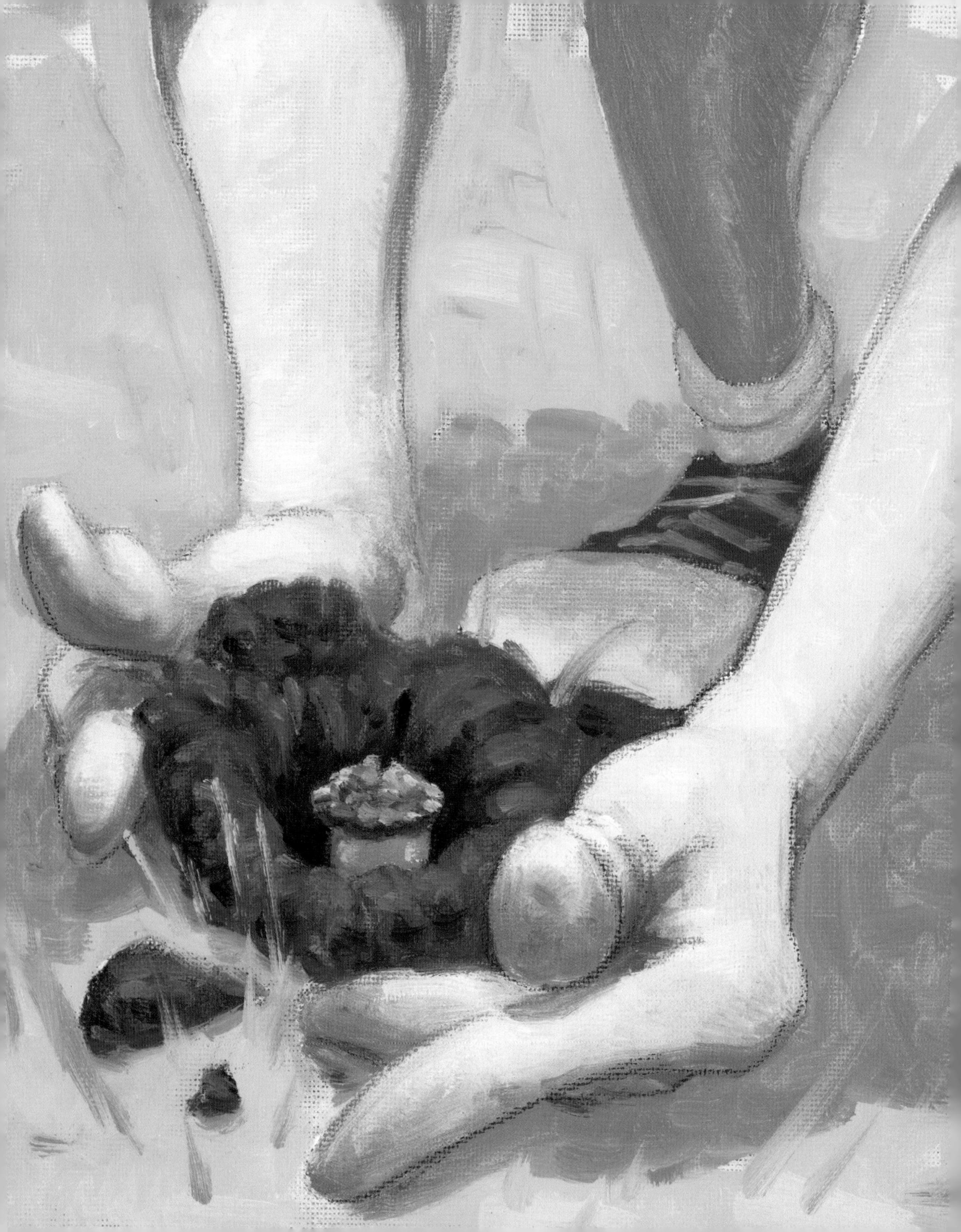

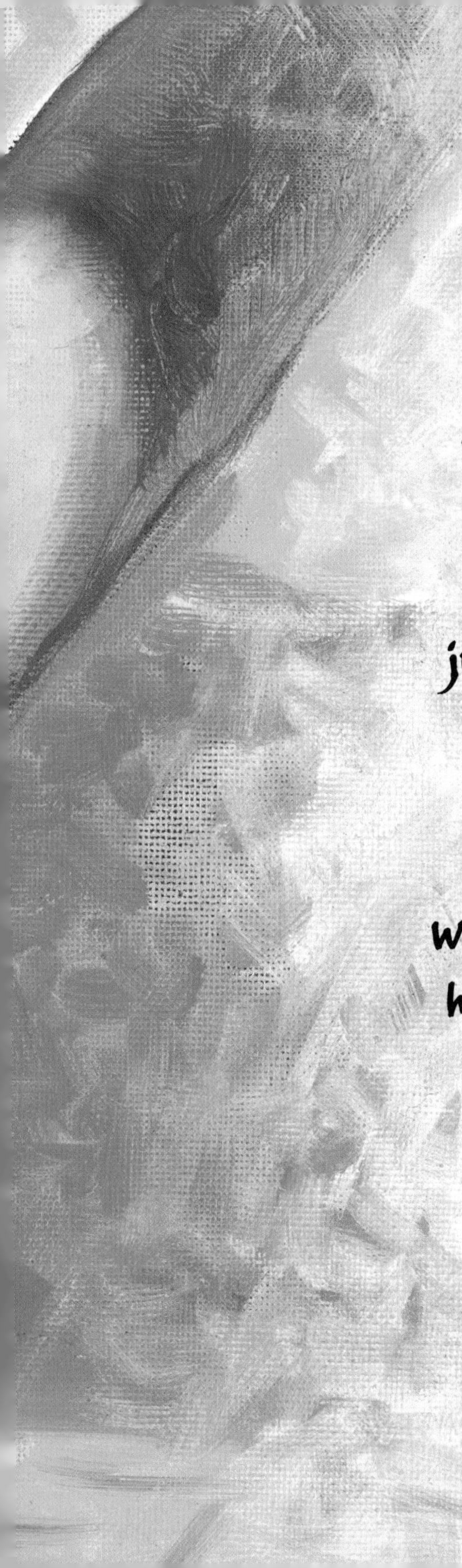

The boy took Lulu to his
backyard and began to
dig a hole. When it was
just big enough, he placed
Lulu in it and covered
her up with dirt.
Even though Lulu felt
warm and safe in the dark
hole, she was very lonely.
WHAT'S HAPPENING?
she wondered.

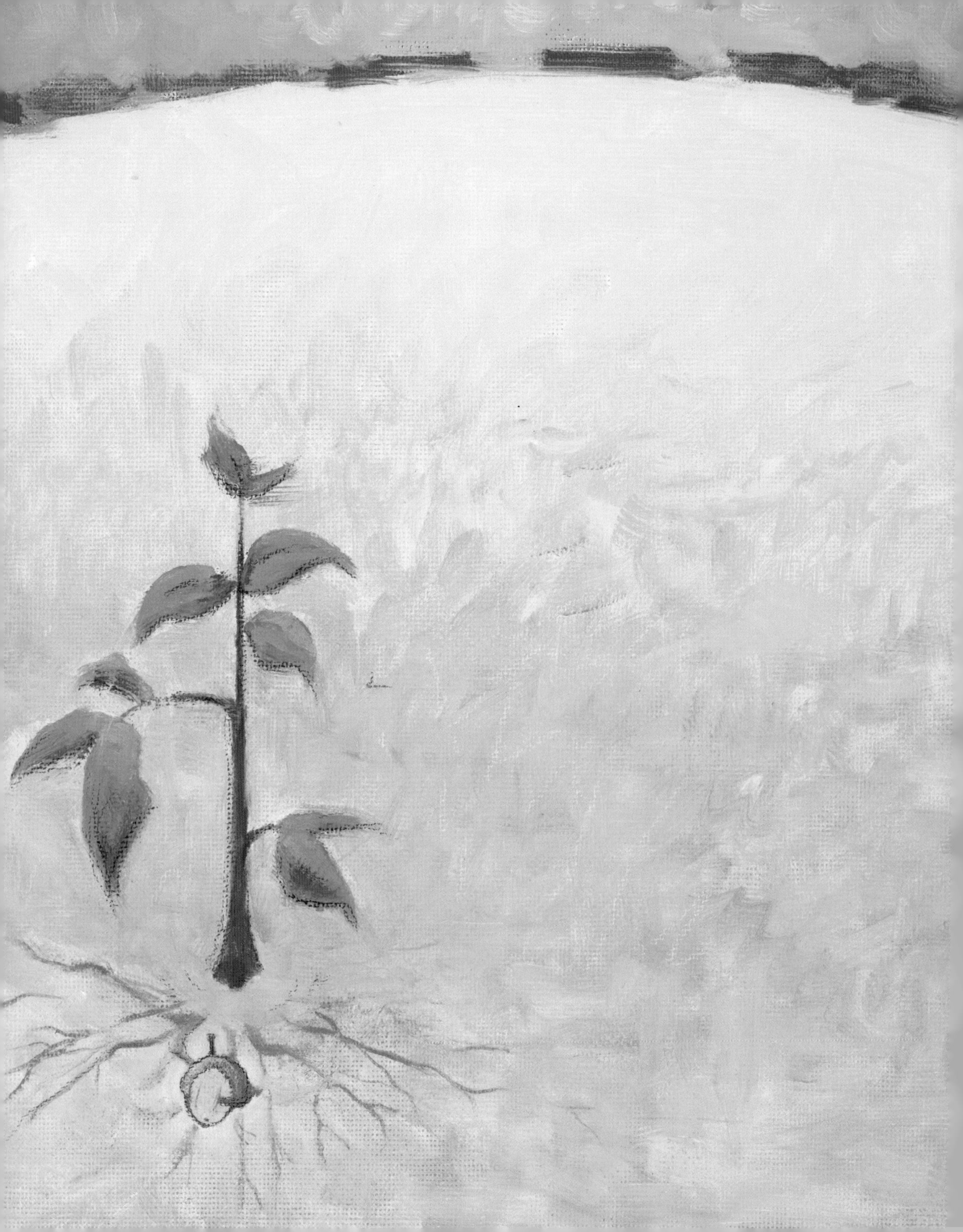

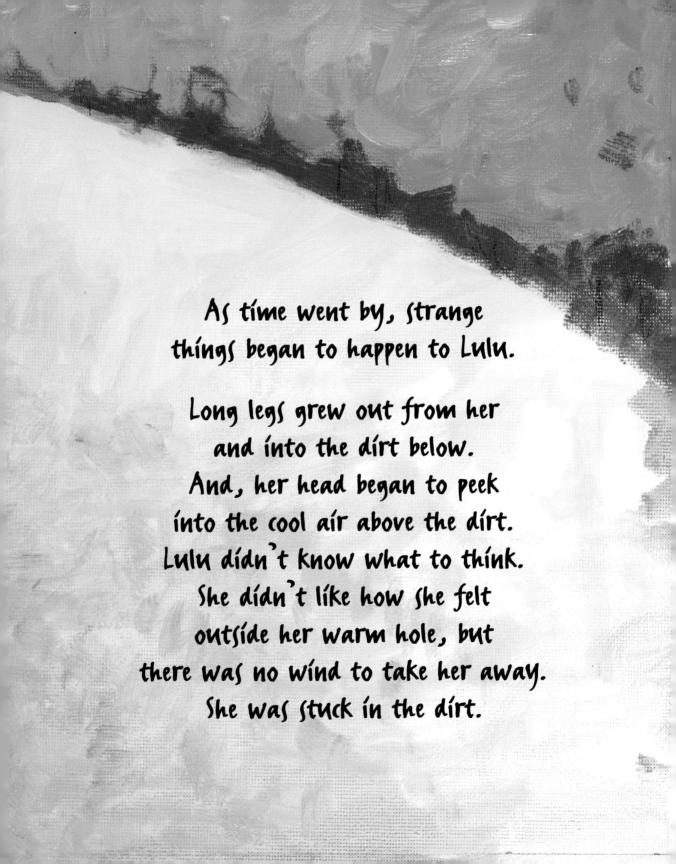

As time went by, strange
things began to happen to Lulu.

Long legs grew out from her
and into the dirt below.
And, her head began to peek
into the cool air above the dirt.
Lulu didn't know what to think.
She didn't like how she felt
outside her warm hole, but
there was no wind to take her away.
She was stuck in the dirt.

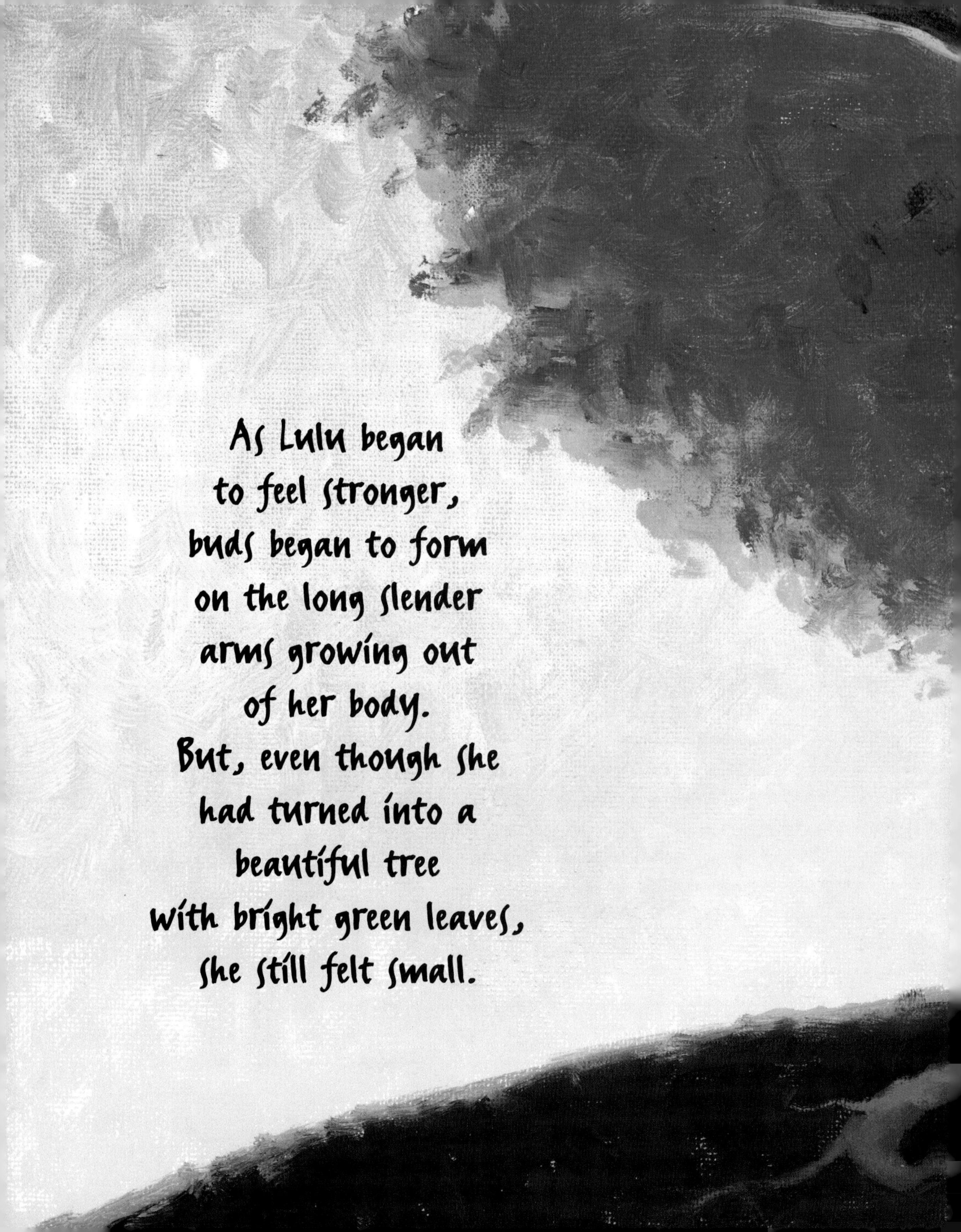

As Lulu began
to feel stronger,
buds began to form
on the long slender
arms growing out
of her body.
But, even though she
had turned into a
beautiful tree
with bright green leaves,
she still felt small.

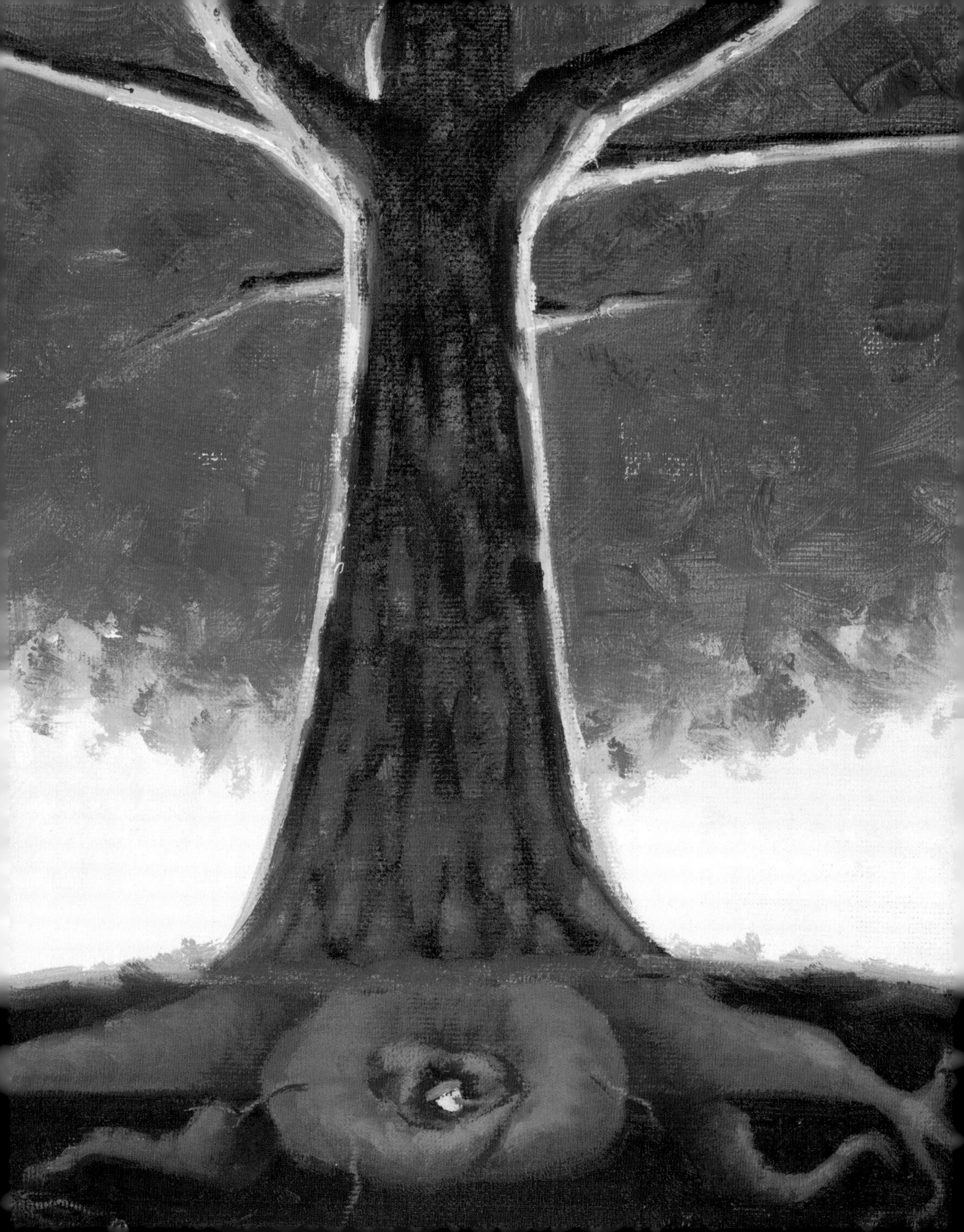

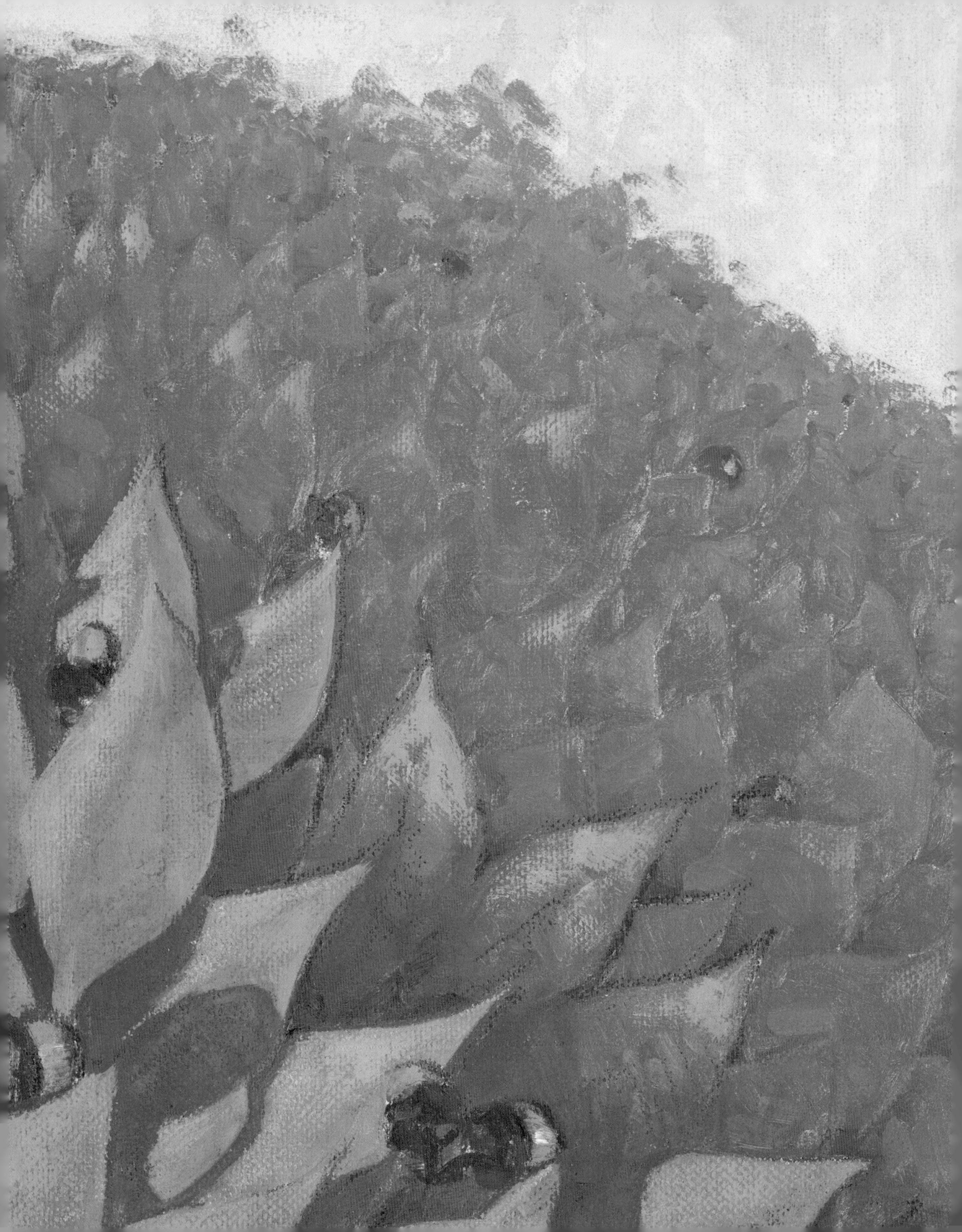

After a long time
had passed, the boy,
now a man, came to
visit her with children
of his own. When Lulu
heard him say, THIS OAK TREE
IS THE MOST BEAUTIFUL OF
ALL GOD'S CREATIONS, her
ears perked up and she became
very excited. She had never
heard herself called that
before. AN OAK TREE,
she thought.
THAT'S ME!

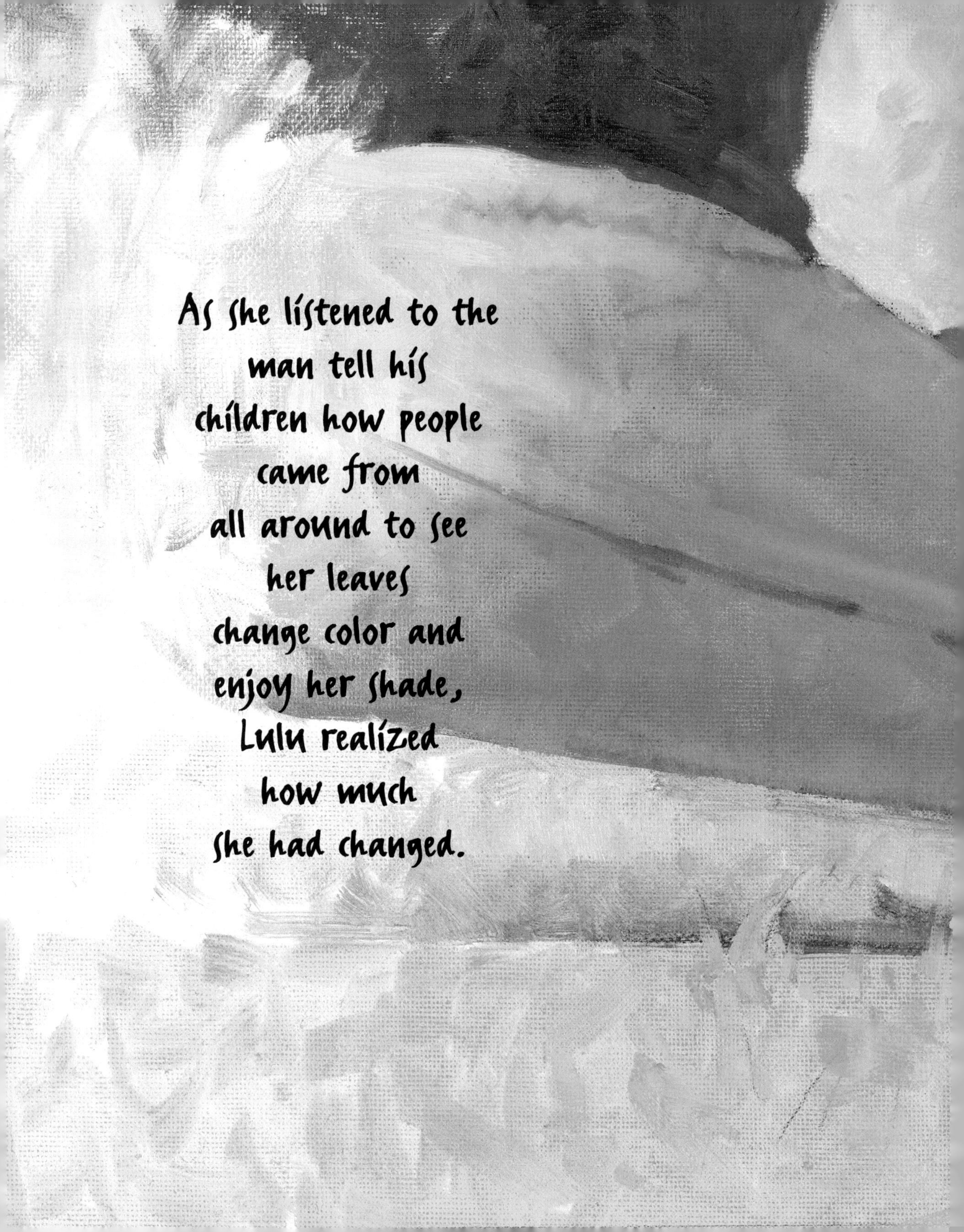

As she listened to the
man tell his
children how people
came from
all around to see
her leaves
change color and
enjoy her shade,
Lulu realized
how much
she had changed.

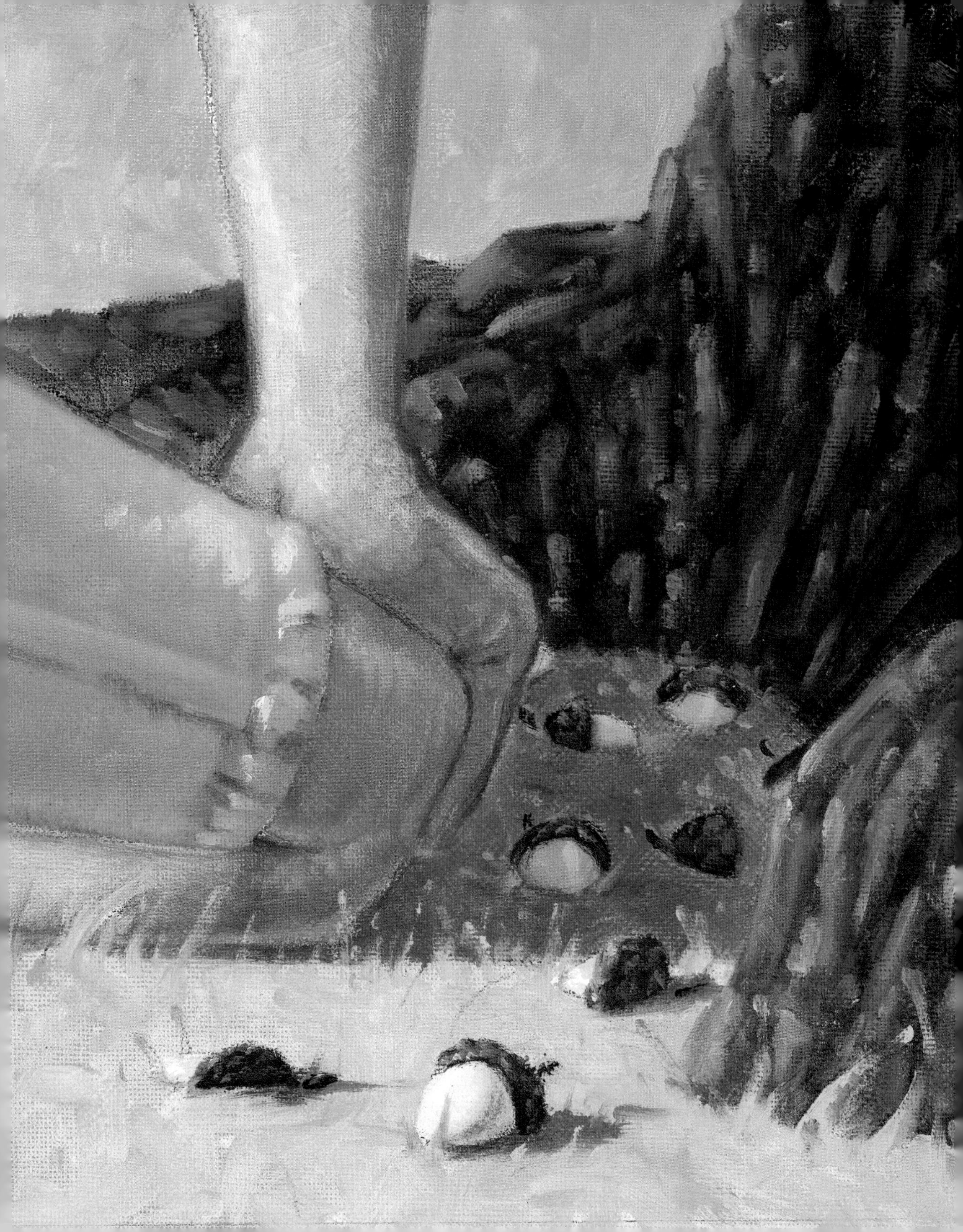

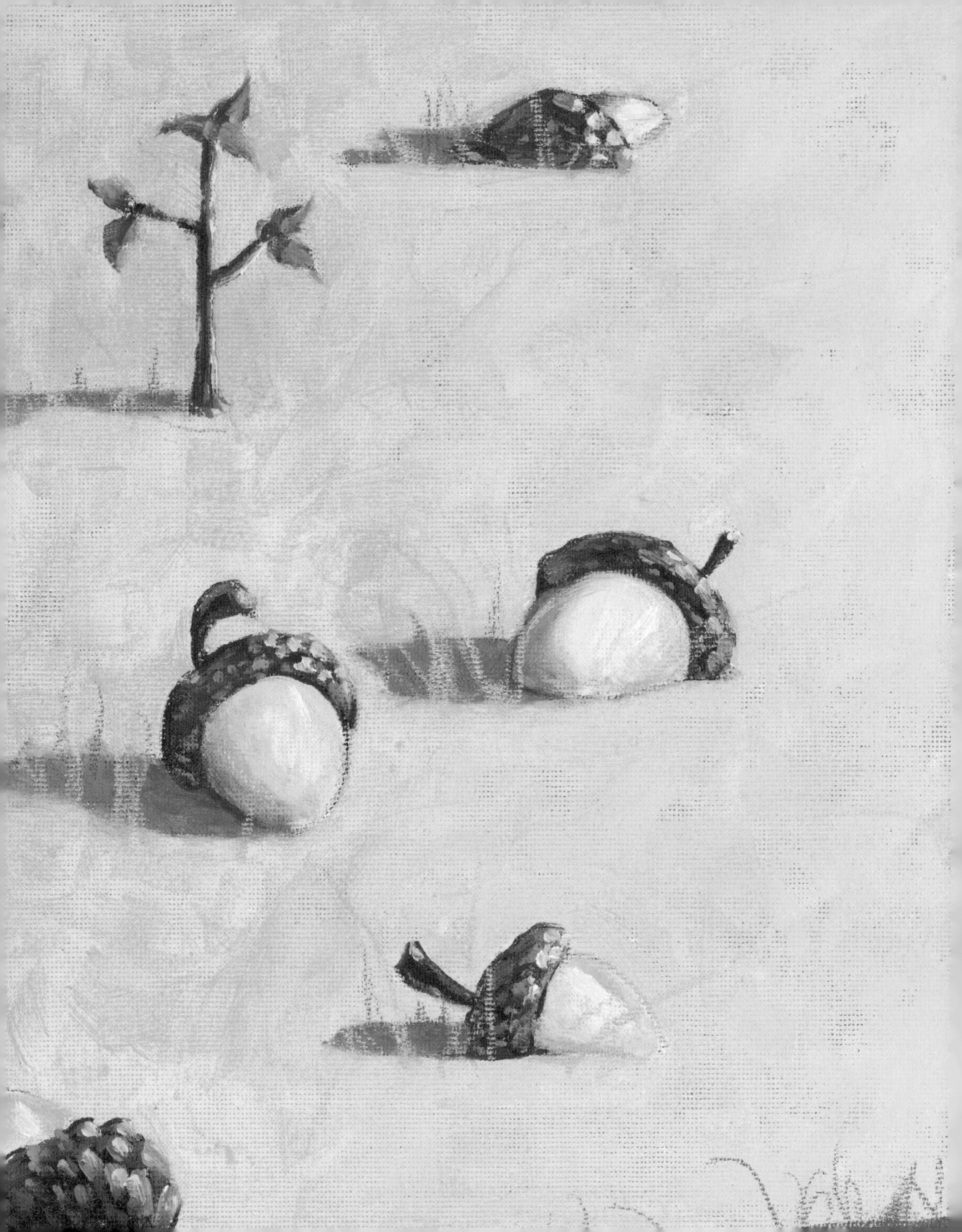

When Lulu finally had
children of her own, she smiled
softly at each one and said,
ONE DAY MY TINY ACORN,
YOU WILL BE A BEAUTIFUL OAK
TREE JUST LIKE ME,
so that they knew how
special they were and never
wondered about all
the wonderful things they
would one day be
able to do, too.

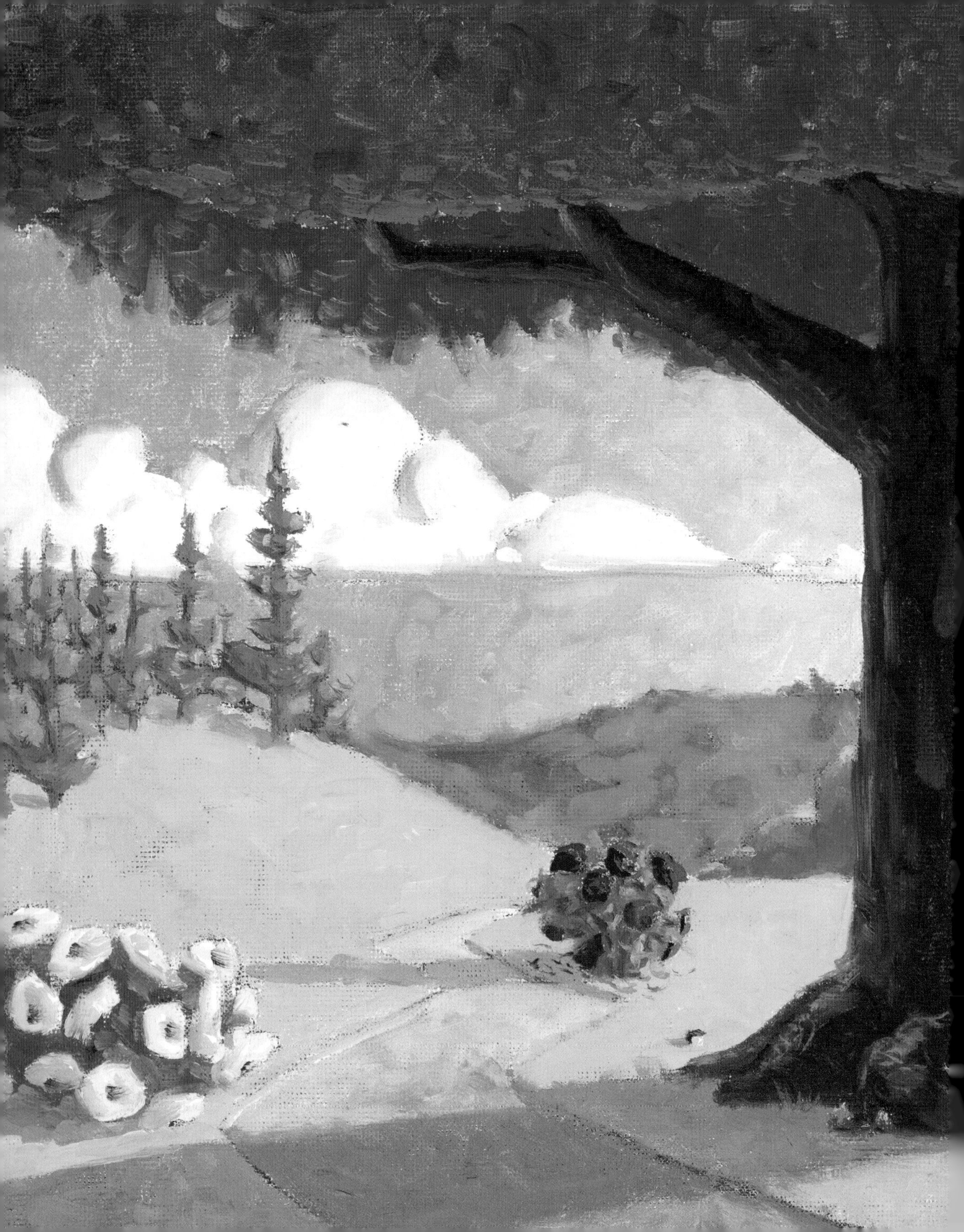

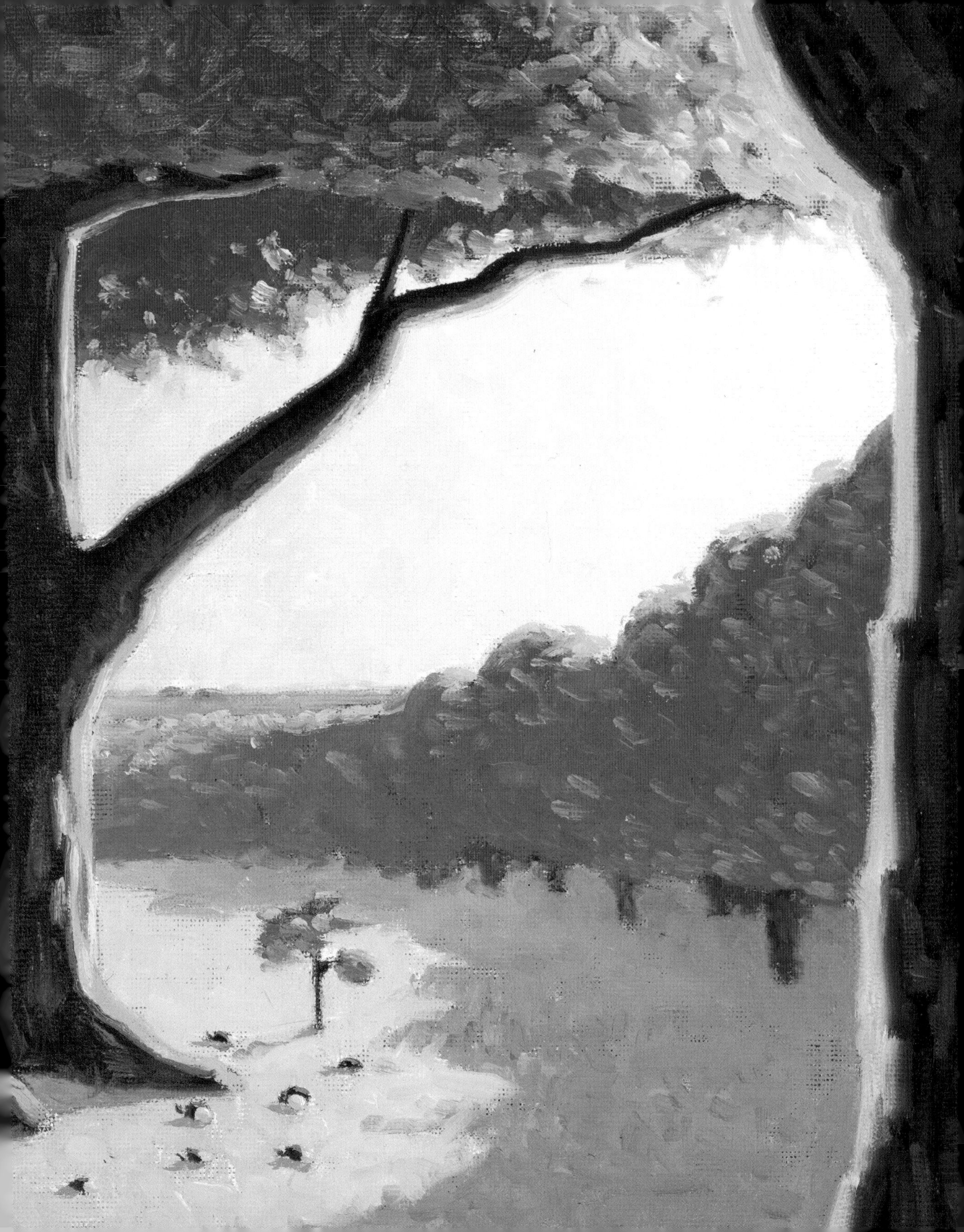

Epilogue

IT WAS ON A COLD NEW ENGLAND NIGHT when the image of Lulu, the tiniest acorn, came to me. I had just moved from New York City to a small town just north of Boston and, although some days I awoke with confidence and enthusiasm for my new life, there were days when the fears and uncertainties I thought I'd left in the city found me, consuming me with worry and self doubt.

Even though, according to the rest of the world, I had accomplished so much—a master's degree from Harvard, degrees from the Sorbonne, the Goethe Institute and the University of Edinburgh, an internship with the United Nations in Geneva, and acceptance into a Ph.D. program at Columbia University—I did not feel successful or fulfilled. I felt like a tiny acorn tossed from place to place, awed at the successes and gifts others seemed to have. I longed to be something more than who I thought I was. Unfortunately, instead of seeing difficulties and personal challenges as necessary growing pains needed in order for me to blossom, I saw roadblocks. When Lulu entered my world, however, she awakened in me a new hope and a new path.

Miraculously, I finished writing *The Tiniest Acorn* and sent it off to a publisher. At about the same time I learned it had been accepted for publication, I had begun to pursue dance professionally, and found the same joy in it as I found in writing. I am now training and teaching in a couple of places near my home, which, if you new me, is quite incredible, considering my lower left leg is missing due to childhood cancer, and I wear a prosthesis (that, of course, is another story for which there is another book).

Please let the sweet story of Lulu, the tiniest acorn, inspire you and your children. And remember, every page turned is another step along the journey leading you to the truth of your own unique brilliance.

Marsha T. Danzig

BOSTON, MA